NAHLA AND THE 3D MACHINE

This book belongs to

....

Written by
Charlene Russell, Joseph Bartlett-Vanderpuye & Nahla-Rose Bartlett-Vanderpuye

Illustrated By Ruxandra Șerbănoiu

It was the turn of the decade, the year 2020.
There were big plans for all, resolutions were plenty.
Two thousand and twenty! Oh, what a ring.
But not a soul knew what it would bring.

In towns and cities across the world,
full of young and wonderous boys and girls.
Who played carefree and stayed amused,
while their parents gasped at the news.

A virus was brewing and rapidly spreading,
and nobody knew which way it was heading.
Life as we knew it was about to be paused.
The government told us to lock all our doors!

Meet Nahla, a young girl who loved to create.
Her heart was as big as the smile on her face.
A problem-solver with a head full of questions,
cheeky ideas, fun jokes, and suggestions.

Every night, once tucked into bed,
when the day was over and her prayers were said,
she would fix her pillow, duvet, and sheets
to make it look like she was still asleep.

Careful not to make a sound,
she grabbed her bedpost and swung around.
Bounced off the walls, to her skateboard. . . **ZOOM**!
Whizzing down the stairs as she left her room.

Faster and quicker the wheels did spin,
aeroplane arms and an excited grin.
Now in the garden - she was getting near.
She stopped her skateboard. "Yes, I'm here!"

Trinkets, devices, gadgets, tools,
paints, tricycles, paddling pools.
Her lab stood before her in all its glory.
Well, it was Dad's shed. . .
But lab sounds better for this story.

With a heart of gold and her thoughts angelic,
and a hand to lend to this newfound pandemic.
What could she do? How would she help?
Her eyes scanned across all the boxes and shelves.

She tapped her foot and rubbed her chin.
The ideas just came tumbling in!
And then it hit her, as if by magic.
"Eureka!" she squealed. That's it, she had it!

With her thinking cap on, she felt instantly wiser.
She'd use Grandma's printer to make up a visor!
On Gran's 3D machine, she'd print off a batch,
choosing blue for the medics. This colour would match.

She had all these big plans, but where would she start?
The panic set in, and she let out a fart.
"Oops!" she exclaimed, then let out a giggle.
She pulled on a lever and gave it a wiggle.

Something was happening! What had she done?
This could be disastrous, but at least it was fun.
The printer was impressive, bold, and pristine
but Nahla didn't know how to use the machine.

While it buzzed and it whirred and it hummed and it clunked,
she was puzzled, concerned, then she mumbled and jumped.
Startled and panicked, she had no one to call,
when an unfamiliar voice echoed off the walls.

"I'd love to be able to print what you need,
but first I require some things to proceed."
Astonished, she looked at the printer in awe,
in disbelief of what she had just heard and saw.

The printer went silent. Nahla was puzzled.
She tried to speak, but her words came out muddled.
She panicked and turned to look back at the house
to make sure nobody had seen her sneak out.

Reassured she was alone in the shed,
she turned to the printer and asked what it said.
"What did you say? Did you just talk?
What else can you do?" Nahla nervously squawked.

"I'm sorry to scare you," the printer said, laughing.
"There's lots I can do, but let's get to masking!
There's something you need to find for me first.
PLA filament - it's kind on the earth."

"PLA filament? Where can I find it?
How much does it cost? Do I need to buy it?
But I have no money!" Nahla's thoughts ran wild.
The questions were many. She paused, then she smiled.

"My piggy bank!" For months she'd been saving.
Mum told her to "save for a day when it's raining."
Dad told her that "money does not grow on trees."
But Gran said, "Oh, darling, just do as you please!"

Nahla wondered to whom she should listen.
Mum, Dad, or Gran? Decisions, decisions. . .
Her mind flashed back to a man on the telly
who said the PPE they need was not ready.

The medics, our heroes, so highly respected,
were fighting this new virus, unprotected.
With a shortage of masks or the right clothing to shield them
whilst nursing our sick men, women, and children.

Nahla jumped on her skateboard and whizzed back to the house,
then crept up the stairs as quiet as a mouse.
Sliding into her room, she grabbed her piggy bank,
jumping out of her skin when it clinked and clanked.

"Sshhh!!!" Nahla hissed. "I'm trying to be quiet.
That PLA filament, I really must buy it!
How much have I saved? Please tell me, please."
She poured out the coins and got down on her knees.

She counted her money. When done, she felt proud.
She excitedly jumped up and shouted out loud,

"Grandma!"

The whole house awoke and flurried.
The unusual shouting made everyone worried.

Grandma in front of Mum, Dad, and her sister.
Half asleep but relieved, they hugged and they kissed her.
"Are you okay, darling?"
"Fifty pounds I've collected
from my piggy bank savings," Nahla interjected.

They glanced at the floor, then back to Nahla, confused.
"I'm going to make masks. I've been watching the news.
I have enough savings to buy what I need.
Grandma, please teach me on your 3D machine."

One little hurdle that Nahla must jump,
the government had ordered all shops to stay shut.
As cash was now void, she swapped coins for Mum's card
and ordered online, straight to her front yard.

She made her return to the shed with a **ZOOM!**
With Grandma this time, landing with a **BOOM!**
The printer stood mighty. They flicked on its switch.
"You came back to find me! I hope you're equipped?"

With lab coats and gloves on, and the filament loaded,
the pair were excited, on the verge of exploding.
With a G-code uploading, impatient they grew,
keen to see just what this printer could do.

They laughed and they joked, made mistakes and kept going.
Grandma's skills, Nahla's keenness, the passion kept flowing.
The whole room was glowing as the first mask was made,
tagged 'You're doing a great job! Love Nahla. Aged 8.'

Hours, then days, the days now a week.
She printed non-stop through home-schooling and sleep.
Then, one day, the most peculiar thing.
The printer just stopped with an almighty **DING!**

Something had happened! What had she done?
This was a disaster and not quite as fun.
A voice came from deep within the machine.
"If you don't feed me, I'll run out of steam."

She glanced at the empty filament in despair,
then paced around the room and slumped in her chair.
"Oh no, it's over!" A tear fell from her eye.
Nahla's plan was on hold. She started to cry.

With her head in her hands, for a moment she stayed,
clueless about how many blue visors she'd made.
Defeated, she stood up to head for the door
but tripped on a box that was left on the floor.

Flustered, Nahla jumped up with a grunt,
expecting to see that same box filled with junk.
But, in actual fact, to the young girl's surprise,
tens of her blue visors sat neatly inside.

She sealed up the package. It was time to donate!
A race against time, but was it too late?
Now for the wait. . . Thoughts ran through her mind.
Did they work? Did they fit? Did they even arrive?

Soon enough, her first batch was received.
The hospital staff were thankful and relieved.
The masks worked, were comfy, and felt safe to use.
Nahla's story travelled, even making the news.

The world stood united, good deeds all around.
Fundraising and baking, new hobbies were found.
Then every Thursday way before it got dark,
people clapped for the NHS at 8 p.m. sharp!

As word spread of what Nahla had done,
requests tumbled in, so she started a fund.
The materials were vital, something Nahla did need,
and the donations made it possible for her to proceed.

Keen to do more, Nahla hurried with haste
to carry on printing but was slowed by the pace.
She couldn't put her finger on it, but something was wrong.
There had to be another way! This was taking too long!

Her headmaster learned of her problems with speed,
so brought her a G-code to quicken her deed.
Plus, a roll of red filament which really looked blazing
and a note that read, "Go Nahla! Amazing!"

That was so kind of him, that really impressed her.
He smiled, waved goodbye, then rode off on his Vespa.
He pinged up the hill. He'd made Nahla's day.
She watched him shrink as he got further away.

Overwhelmed with excitement to try her new kit,
to the shed Nahla cartwheeled, landing in the splits.
The code was amazing! Her printing time halved.
"There's no stopping you now," said the printer, who laughed.

Hours, then days, the days turned to weeks.
She'd been at it for months and was reaching her peak.
In surgeries and care homes, her masks were worn.
She even donated to the hospital where she was born.

As dusk fell, she and the printer sat in the shed.
In the background, a voice on the radio said,
"breaking news! The official PPE has arrived
for all medical workers!" The voice then advised.

An emotional Nahla stared at the machine.
"Our job here is done. We've made such a great team!"
The printer groaned but lacked its usual conversation.
Could their talks have been a slice of her imagination?

Now feeling alone, Nahla started her last visor.
She then saw her little sister watching, which surprised her!
Both feeling proud, with full hearts and tired heads,
when done, they hugged each other, then they made their way to bed.

The following morning marked a brand-new beginning.
Nahla, still bleary-eyed with her head still spinning,
sat and watched TV, lounging on the sofa.
The news then announced that the lockdown was over!

Rainbows shot through the sky! The pandemic, now shifting.
Kids flocked to the playground because restrictions were lifting.
They'd all found their brilliance whilst forced to stay home.
Every cloud has a silver lining, so it is known.

Their minds had no boundaries, and their dreams knew no end.
It only made sense they'd become the best of friends.
A collection of talents, the 'Futures' by name,
who planned to meet weekly by the brown climbing frame.

Feeling inspired, telling jokes, and asking questions,
sharing ideas, never short of new suggestions.
They all chimed together, "The future is bright!"
They say the brightest of stars, shine on the darkest of nights.

GLOSSARY

3D Printer: A machine that creates a physical object by repeatedly laying down many thin layers to create one larger 3D model. The first 3D printer was invented by an engineer named Charles (Chuck) Hull in 1984.

Decade: A period of ten years.

G-code: Stands for geometric code. It is a programming language used to tell a computer what to do and how to do it.

Government: An organised group of people who work together to decide how a country should be run.

Medic: A person who works in the medical field (i.e. a doctor or nurse), whose responsibility it is to help people with illnesses.

NHS: An abbreviation for the 'National Health Service'. The publicly funded healthcare system in England.

Pandemic: A new or changed disease that affects a huge area of the world or the whole world at one time.

PLA Filament: A biodegradable (Earth-friendly) plastic-like material, made from natural materials like corn starch or sugarcane. It can be melted down and moulded by a 3-D printer to make products.

PPE: An abbreviation for personal protective equipment. This makes reference to protective masks, clothing, helmets, goggles, or other garments/equipment designed to protect the wearer's body from infection or injury.

Virus: An infectious particle which multiplies itself when it finds the right place to do so (i.e. in humans, animals, etc).

Vespa: An Italian brand of motor scooters. The name means 'Wasp' in Italian.

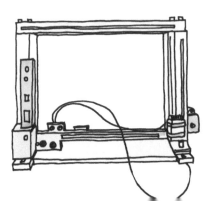

This book was inspired and co-written by Nahla-Rose Bartlett-Vanderpuye, who made hundreds of 3D printed visors using her grandma's 3D printer and her own pocket money. These visors were then donated to the National Health Service (NHS) at the height of the Covid-19 pandemic.

This book is dedicated to our wonderful NHS and to all whom the Covid-19 crisis impacted.

With an extra special thanks to my wonderful STEM-crazy Grandma Rose, 'Rock-Off' sister Zuri, & my beautiful baby brother Kenzo. Not forgetting all the incredible people across the world who were also 3D printing for the same cause.

** In loving memory of my Grandad Roy **

Xx

• • • •

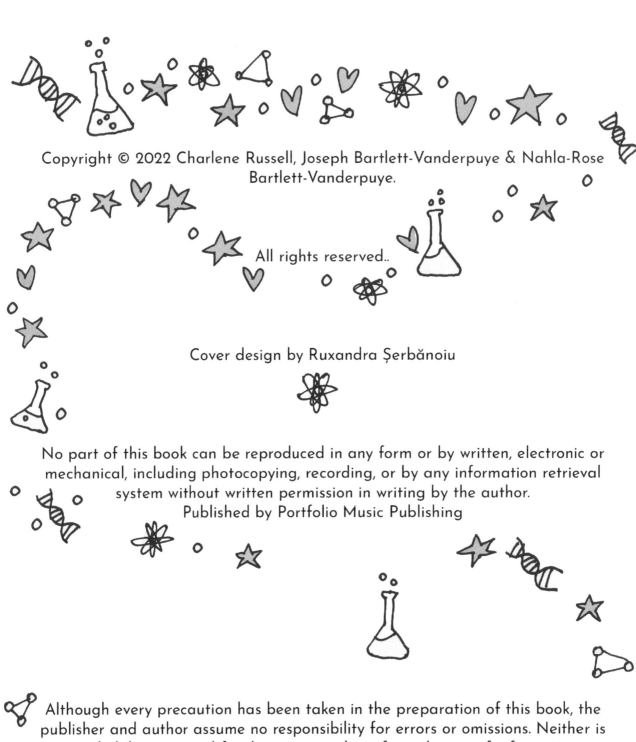

CPSIA information can be obtained
at www.ICGtesting.com
Printed in the USA
BVHW022215061122
651324BV00003B/7